Fruit Salad:

A first look at fruit

Julia Eccleshare

Illustrated by Martin Ursell

Hamish Hamilton · London

5224134 634

First published in Great Britain 1986 by
Hamish Hamilton Children's Books
27 Wrights Lane, London W8 5TZ
Copyright © 1986 by Julia Eccleshare (text)
Copyright © 1986 by Martin Ursell (illustrations)

Designed by Miriam Yarrien

British Library Cataloguing in Publication Data

Eccleshare, Julia
Fruit salad.
1. Fruit – Juvenile literature
I. Title
634   TX397

ISBN 0–241–11796–8

Printed in Great Britain by
Cambus Litho, East Kilbride

Contents

Orange   6

Pawpaw   8

Fig   10

Banana   12

Water Melon   14

Lychee   16

Raspberry   18

Mango   20

Kiwi Fruit   22

Avocado Pear   24

Pineapple   26

Index   28

Orange

Oranges grow on trees which have thick, dark-green leaves and white, sweet-smelling flowers.

Orange trees grow in Mediterranean countries where it is warm and sunny.

The skin or peel of an orange is leathery and oily. The inner flesh is the part we eat. It is full of sugar and juice. Both the peel and the flesh are orange in colour.

Oranges can be squeezed to produce a delicious juice that is drunk all over the world.

Pawpaw

The proper name for a pawpaw is a 'papaya'. It grows in the Bahamas, West Indies and South Africa.

The pawpaw tree has lovely green leaves and dark-red flowers. Pawpaw fruits are oval or round. They have green skins, which turn yellow or orange when ripe. We eat the flesh,

which is pink or orange with hundreds of little
grey-black seeds in the middle.

Pawpaw can be eaten with meat, but it is
tastiest sliced and sprinkled
with lime juice for breakfast.
Why don't you try some?

Fig

Figs are browny-green or purple when ripe.
They have wrinkly skins which can be eaten
with the insides. The inside of a fig is made
up of hundreds and hundreds of little seeds.

Figs grow in Mediterranean countries, on
trees with wide-spreading woody branches
and thick, grey-green leaves.

The fruit is sweet and sticky. Figs can be
eaten fresh or dried.

Banana

Bananas grow on trees up to six metres high, which are topped by huge leaves.

Bananas grow from the flowers in bunches or 'hands'. Each hand is made up of a group of fingers. These are the bananas themselves. The bananas grow upwards. There may be as many as fifty or a hundred bananas in a bunch.

Banana trees grow in Africa, Central America and the Canary Islands.

Bananas have a thick peel which is yellow when ripe. Inside, the flesh is soft and white. They may be eaten raw, or cooked with meat, or in puddings.

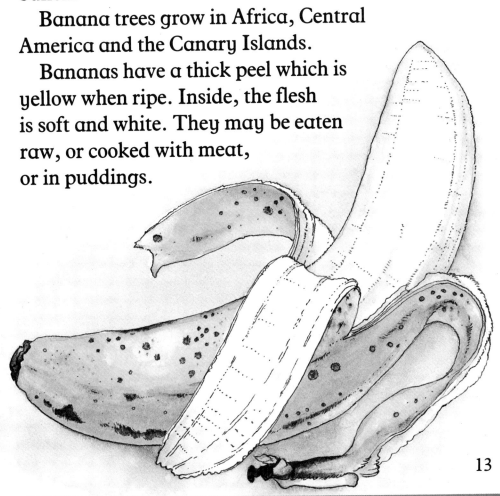

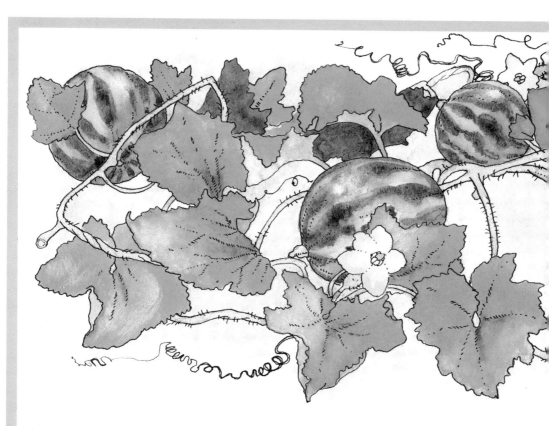

Water Melon

Water melons are huge and round. Their skins are dark-green and hard. The flesh inside is a beautiful pink colour. There are hundreds of black seeds in the middle of the melon.

Water melons grow in Africa and Mediterranean countries. They grow on vines

that creep along the ground, with green
leaves and pale-yellow flowers.

In hot countries, water melons are sold in
slices as a refreshing snack. They
are very thirst-quenching.
Try eating a slice of water
melon in the summer.

Lychee

Lychees were first grown in China, and they are still popular as a pudding at the end of a Chinese meal. Nowadays they are also grown

in Israel, Mauritius, South Africa
and parts of America.

Lychee trees grow up to twelve
metres high, and the lychees grow
off them in bunches.

The fruit is plum-sized and has
a rough skin which is pinky-brown.
The skin cannot be eaten. The
flesh is white, and has a sweet
flavour. At the centre of the
fruit there is a glossy
brown seed.

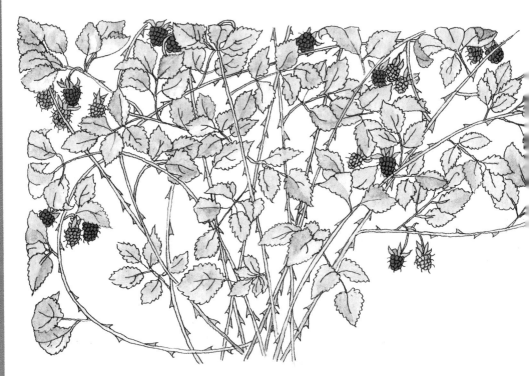

Raspberry

Raspberries grow on bushes. Each bush is about two metres high. The leaves are green, and the flowers whitish-yellow. The raspberries hang from the branches. The berries themselves are a beautiful pinky-red when ripe. They are made up of lots of little seeds clustered around a central core.

Raspberries grow in damp, cool climates. Scotland is the best place in the world for growing raspberries.

They are tastiest eaten raw on their own or in a fruit salad.

Mango

Mangoes are often said to be the world's most
delicious fruit.
They grow in India
and Burma.

Mangoes grow on tall, evergreen trees which may be as much as twenty metres high. The flowers are small, pink and sweet-smelling. Mango fruit is round or oval. The skin is usually a greenish-yellow colour, but is sometimes bright red. Inside the skin there is a single seed with juicy, yellowy-orange flesh around it.

Mangoes are difficult to eat. They are full of sticky juice which spurts out when you cut into them. Mangoes can be mixed with other fruits to make a delicious fruit salad.

21

Kiwi Fruit

Kiwi fruit are really called 'Chinese gooseberries'. This is because they first came from China. They now grow in New Zealand, and have been nicknamed 'kiwi fruit'.

They grow on vines with green leaves and pale-yellow flowers. In shape and size the fruit are like rather large eggs.

Kiwi fruit have a thin peel which is browny-green and slightly hairy. The peel can be eaten with the flesh. The flesh is emerald-green with edible black seeds dotted about in it.

Kiwi fruit are delicious eaten raw in slices.

Avocado Pear

Avocado pears have hard, green or brown skins and soft, pale-green flesh. At the centre they have a large stone.

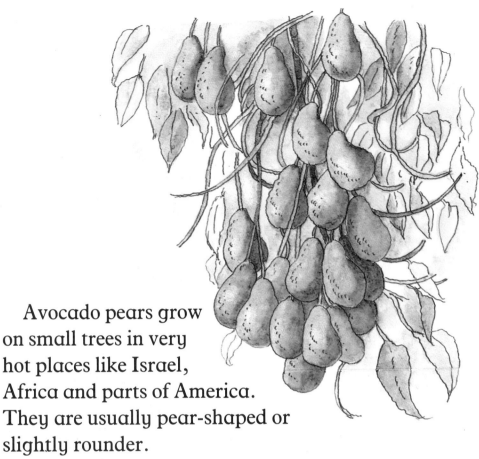

Avocado pears grow
on small trees in very
hot places like Israel,
Africa and parts of America.
They are usually pear-shaped or
slightly rounder.

The skin of the pear cannot be eaten, but
the flesh is rich and buttery. It is often
served with an oil and vinegar sauce,
and can also be mixed with crispy
bacon to make a tasty sandwich filling.

Pineapple

A pineapple grows upwards from the centre of a bush with hard, spiky leaves.

The skin of the pineapple is thick and

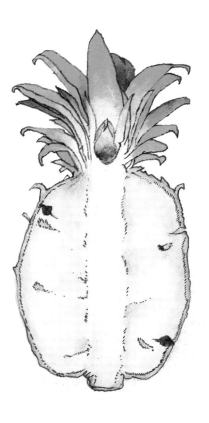

brown. It protects the yellow flesh inside. The flesh is chewy and full of juice.

Pineapples grow in very hot places like Hawaii, Australia, Africa and Cuba.

Pineapple flesh can be eaten with meat and vegetables in curries. It can also be eaten as a refreshing fruit at the end of a meal.

Index

A

Africa	13, 14, 25, 27
America	17, 25
Australia	27
Avocado pear	24–25

B

Bahamas	8
Banana	12–13
Burma	20
Bush – pineapple	26
– raspberry	18

C

Canary Islands, The	13
Central America	13
China	16, 22
Chinese gooseberries	22
Cuba	27

F

Fig	10–11

H

Hawaii	27

I

India	20
Israel	17, 25

K

Kiwi fruit	22–23

L

Lychee	16–17

M

Mango	20–21
Mauritius	17
Mediterranean countries	6, 10, 14

N

New Zealand | 22

O

Orange | 6–7

P

Papaw | 8–9
Papaya | 8
Pineapple | 26–27

R

Raspberry | 18–19

S

Scotland | 19
South Africa | 8, 17

T

Tree – avocado | 25
    – banana | 12, 13
    – fig | 10
    – lychee | 17
    – mango | 21
    – orange | 6
    – pawpaw | 8

V

Vines – kiwi fruit | 23
    – water melon | 14

W

Water melon | 14–15
West Indies | 8